P9-CQI-504

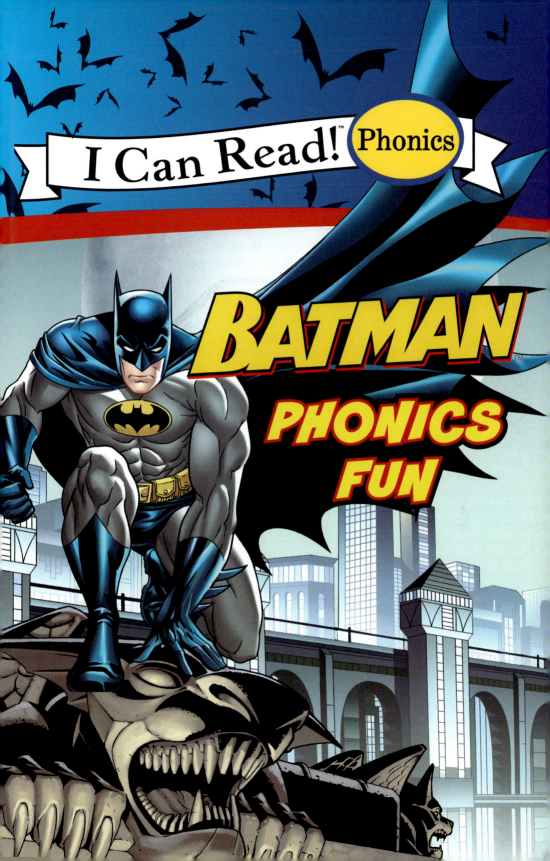

I Can Read Book® is a trademark of HarperCollins Publishers.
Batman: Meet the Super Heroes
Batman: Feline Felonies
Batman: The Mayhem of Metallo
Batman: The Dragon Disaster
Batman: Gotham's Villains Unleashed
Batman: Batman's Foes
Batman: Meet Batman
Batman: Toxic Terror
Batman: Batman's Friends
Batman: Batman's Gadgets
Batman: Batman's Vehicles
Batman: See the Batcave

Copyright © 2011 DC Comics.
BATMAN, SUPERMAN, and WONDER WOMAN are trademarks and © DC Comics.
(s11)
HARP2627

BATMAN created by Bob Kane
SUPERMAN created by Jerry Siegel and Joe Shuster
WONDER WOMAN created by William Moulton Marston.

All rights reserved. Manufactured in China.
No part of this book may be used or reproduced
in any manner whatsoever without written permission except
in the case of brief quotations embodied in critical articles and reviews.
For information address HarperCollins Children's Books,
a division of HarperCollins Publishers,
195 Broadway, New York, NY 10007.
www.icanread.com

First Edition

15 16 17 SCP 10 9 8 7 6 5 4

Table of Contents

Letter to Parents

Dear Parents,

Your child is about to start an exciting adventure. He or she is going to learn to read. By choosing your child's favorite characters, you have already accomplished something very important—motivation!

Batman Phonics Fun includes twelve storybooks, planned by a phonics expert. The books are intended for children to read at home with a parent or caregiver and, eventually, by themselves.

- *Batman Phonics Fun* introduces long and short vowel sounds. One of the key components in becoming a fluent reader is practice, so this set features one book for each sound, plus one introductory story and one book that reinforces all the sounds. Learning to read long and short vowels is rewarding because they are found everywhere!
- Fun Batman words have been included to make the stories rich and enjoyable.
- The stories also include sight words. These are words frequently found in books that can be hard to sound out. They just need to be learned by sight!
- Picture clues support the text in each story and help children learn new words.

As children master the sounds and words, they will gain experience and confidence in their ability to understand sounds, sound out words, and READ! Here are some suggestions for using *Batman Phonics Fun* to help your child on the road to reading:

1. Read the books aloud to your child. The first time you read a story, read it all the way through. Then invite your child to follow along by pointing out words as you read them. Encourage him or her to try to sound out new words that use familiar sounds, or that are pictured in the illustrations.

2. Discuss each sound found on the first page with your child. Help your child sound out the new words in the story. Demonstrate the vowel sounds—for example, by telling your child that the short **o** vowel sound is found in the word **hot**.

3. Look at the pictures with your child. Encourage him or her to tell the story through the pictures. Point out objects in the pictures and ask your child to name them.

We hope that you and your child enjoy *Batman Phonics Fun*, and that it is the start of many happy reading adventures.

The HarperCollins Editors

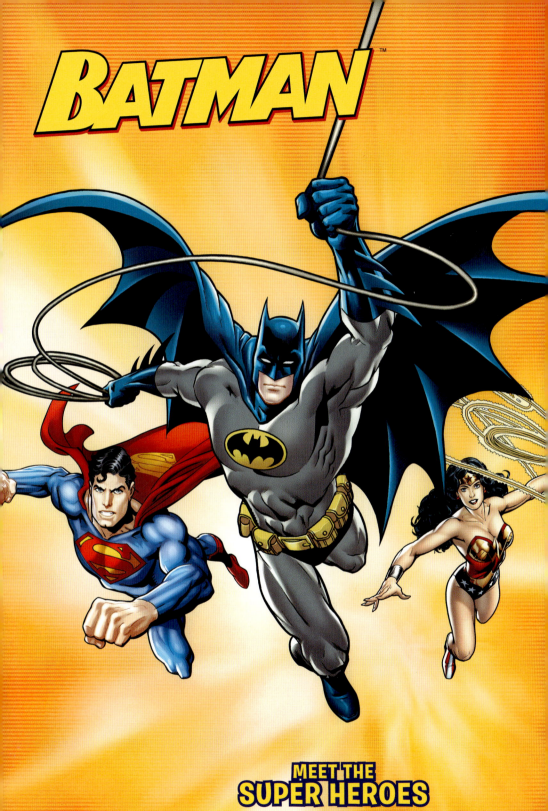

BATMAN™

MEET THE
SUPER HEROES

Book 1 • Introduction

In this story you will learn new sight words.
Can you find these words?

also	and	can
has	he	him
if	in	is
lots	of	on
she	that	these

Here are some fun Batman words:

Amazon	friends	powers
princess	vision	

Batman has two super hero
friends that he really trusts.

Superman lives in Metropolis.

But he is always nearby

if Batman needs him.

Superman has lots of powers.

He has X-ray vision and

super-speed.

And he can fly!

Wonder Woman is an

Amazon princess.

She is very strong.

Wonder Woman can also
talk to animals!

Batman can always count
on these friends.

In this story you will learn about the **short a** vowel sound. Can you find these words and sound them out?

and	**asked**	**at**
attack	**Batman**	**catnap**
cats	**Catwoman**	**fast**
gas	**grab**	**have**
laughed	**plan**	**scratched**
that's	**tracked**	

a	**for**	**from**	**he**	**of**
the	**their**	**to**	**were**	

Here are some fun Batman words:

bomb	**cloud**	**criminals**

Batman tracked two criminals dressed like cats:

Catwoman and the Cheetah.

Batman asked

Wonder Woman for help.

"I have a plan," he said.

Catwoman and the Cheetah

wanted to grab a tiger

from the zoo.

"Not so fast." said Batman.

The feline foes scratched at
Batman and Wonder Woman.
But the super heroes
were ready for their attack.

Batman threw a smoke bomb.

A cloud of sleeping gas
covered the cats.

"That's some catnap!"

the heroes laughed.

BATMAN™

THE MAYHEM OF METALLO

Book 3 • Short e

In this story you will learn about the **short e** vowel sound. Can you find these words and sound them out?

better	chest	end
enemy	friend	get
help	menace	mess
metal	next	pest
rescue	sends	

Here are some sight words:

a	an	at	he	his
in	is	of	that	the
they	this	to		

Here are some fun Batman words:

knocks	kryptonite	trouble

Superman is Batman's friend.

Metallo is Superman's enemy.

Metallo keeps kryptonite
inside his chest.

Superman is in trouble!

He needs help

to beat this pest.

Batman swoops to the rescue!

"I must get that kryptonite,"

he says.

Batman sends a hook flying.

"Time to put an end

to this mess," he says.

The hook knocks the kryptonite
out of Metallo's chest.
Superman is okay.

"Better luck next time!"

they laugh at the metal menace.

In this story you will learn about the **short i** vowel sound. Can you find these words and sound them out?

big	bit	bring
city	did	disappear
grin	his	in
it	it's	linked
pitched	signal	this
with		

Here are some sight words:

a	can	he	the
through	to	was	we

Here are some fun Batman words:

Batrope	dragon

Bruce Wayne did not

believe his eyes.

A big dragon flew over the city.

"How did this happen?" he said.

Batman pitched his Batrope
at the dragon.
The dragon bit
right through it.

Batman needed help.

He sent a signal to his friends.

"We can bring this dragon down together," said Batman.

Soon, the dragon was trapped.

Wonder Woman linked minds

with the dragon.

She told it to disappear.

The dragon was gone in no time!

"It's good to have friends like you,"
Batman said with a grin.

In this story you will learn about the **short o** vowel sound. Can you find these words and sound them out?

block	**cops**	**copter**
drop	**got**	**Gotham**
hop	**hot**	**job**
mob	**not**	**on**
robbing	**Robin**	**stop**
unlocked		

Here are some sight words:

a	**and**	**have**	**him**
his	**in**	**into**	**it**
of	**the**	**them**	**to**
was			

Here are some fun Batman words:

Arkham	**asylum**	**criminals**
laser		

The Joker unlocked the gates
to Arkham Asylum.
A mob of criminals
was loose in Gotham!

Batman and Robin got the
terrible news.
"We have to stop them!"
said Robin.

Two-Face was robbing the bank.

"Drop the money!" yelled Batman.

"You're not going anywhere!"

Mr. Freeze turned Robin

into a block of ice.

"It's about to get hot in here,"

said Batman.

His laser melted the ice.

The Penguin tried to escape

on his umbrella-copter.

Batman grabbed him.

"Back to prison, Penguin.

Hop to it!"

"We've done our job,"

said Batman and Robin.

"Time to leave you with the cops!"

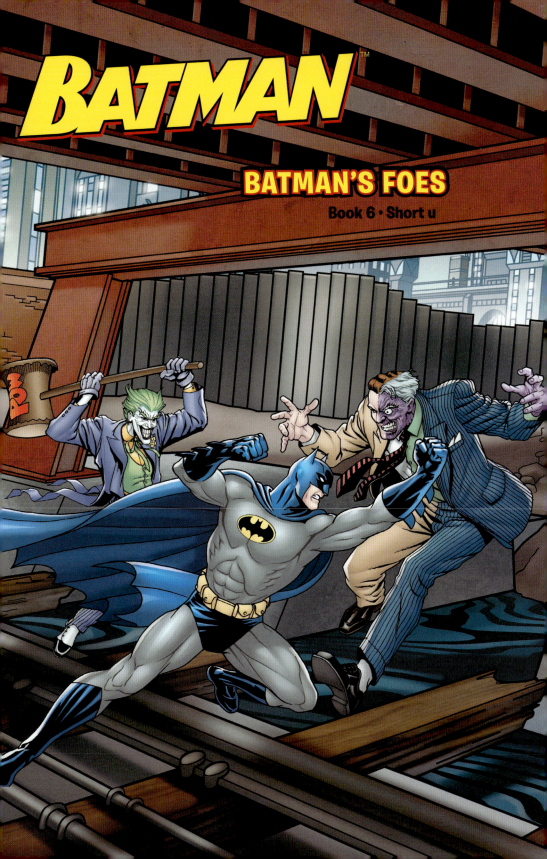

In this story you will learn about the **short u** vowel sound. Can you find these words and sound them out?

bunch	**but**	**funny**
hunt	**jump**	**jungle**
just	**luck**	**none**
pun	**pulls**	**stun**
thumb	**touch**	**under**
up		

Here are some sight words:

a	**an**	**and**	**are**	**can**
for	**is**	**it**	**of**	**she**
these	**to**	**with**		

Here are some fun Batman words:

action   **control**   **deadly**   **villains**

Batman's enemies

are an evil bunch.

It is up to him to keep them

under control.

The Joker loves a good pun.

He pulls a lot of pranks,

but none of them is funny.

Two-Face flips a coin

to choose between good and bad.

He likes to leave things

up to luck.

Mr. Freeze's ray can stun
anyone that tries to hunt him.

Poison Ivy is known

for her green thumb.

She can make a jungle turn

deadly with just one touch.

Batman sees these villains.

Time to jump into action!

In this story you will learn about the **long a** vowel sound. Can you find these words and sound them out?

afraid	Batcave	brave
cape	case	chase
day	making	name
place	races	safe
save	Wayne	

Here are some sight words:

a	and	be	can	is
it	on	the	to	

Here are some fun Batman words:

Gotham	scary	scene
suit	trouble	

Gotham City can be a scary place.

It's Batman's job to keep it safe.

Batman's name
is Bruce Wayne.
Bruce is very brave.

Bruce sees the Bat-Signal.

A bad guy must be making trouble.

Bruce is on the case!

Bruce runs to the Batcave.

He puts on his suit and cape.

Now he is Batman!

Batman races to the crime scene.

He is ready to chase the bad guy.

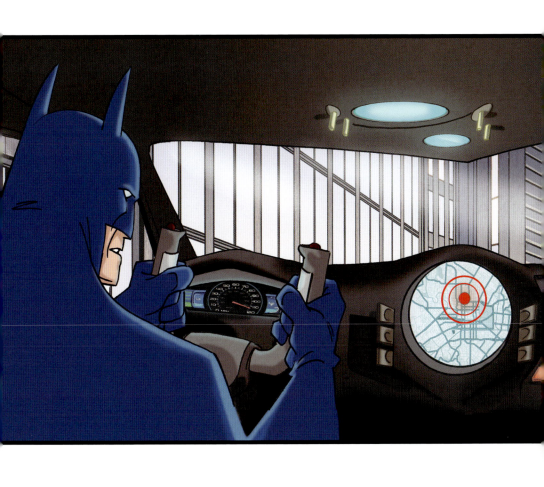

Batman is not afraid.

It is up to him to save the day.

BATMAN™

TOXIC TERROR

Book 8 • Long e

In this story you will learn about the **long e** vowel sound. Can you find these words and sound them out?

breathing	easily	evil	freed
freeze	green	he	here
Ivy	leave	please	people
reach	schemes	secret	see
speed	tree	trees	

Here are some sight words:

a	and	are	at	him
his	in	into	of	the
then	this	to		

Here are some fun Batman words:

costume   Gotham's   poison

"Master Wayne, look here, please," said Alfred. "You must see this!"

"People are turning into trees," said Bruce.

"Sounds like one of Poison Ivy's evil schemes."

Bruce changed into

his secret costume.

He drove the Batmobile at top

speed to reach Gotham's park.

"Freeze," said Batman.

"Oh, Batman," said Poison Ivy. "Why can't you make like a tree and leave?"

Ivy sprayed Batman.

His mask kept him from

breathing in the green gas.

Batman stopped Ivy easily.

Then he freed all the people!

BATMAN™

BATMAN'S FRIENDS

Book 9 • Long i

In this story you will learn about the **long i** vowel sound. Can you find these words and sound them out?

allies	by	crime
disguise	fight	find
guys	hide	knight
life	night	ride
right	shines	side
sky	time	

Here are some sight words:

and	has	into	they
from	how	these	to
his	there	for	
the	but	him	
are	he	is	

Here are some fun Batman words:

Commissioner   Gotham's   trouble

Bruce Wayne is Batman,

Gotham's Dark Knight.

He protects the city from crime.

But even Batman needs help

from time to time.

Luckily, he has friends by his side.

Alfred is Bruce's oldest friend.

Bruce has known him all his life.

Alfred helps hide Bruce's disguise.

Robin and Batman

fight Gotham's bad guys.

Whenever there is trouble,

Robin is always there for the ride.

Commissioner Gordon knows
how to find Batman.
He shines the Bat-Signal
into the night sky.

These are Batman's trusted allies.

They help him fight for what is right!

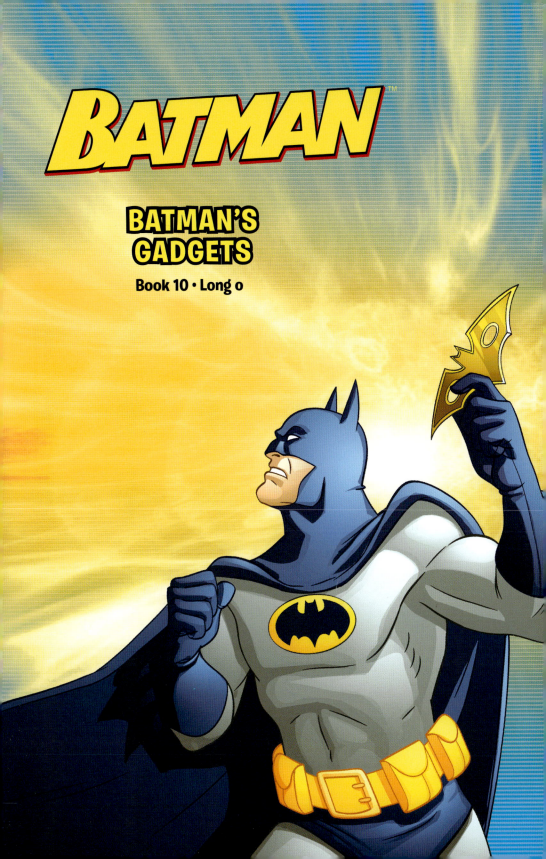

In this story you will learn about the **long o** vowel sound. Can you find these words and sound them out?

alone	arrows	blow
clothes	cold	foe
glow	goes	knows
no	roll	rope
shows	smoke	throws
toes		

Here are some sight words:

a	and	are
as	is	that
the	through	to

Here are some fun Batman words:

Batarangs	darkness	gadgets
ordinary	vision	

Batman knows that strength
alone can't beat a foe.
He needs his gadgets with him
when he goes to fight crime.

Batman's mask
makes his eyes glow.
His night vision shows him how
to move through the darkness.

Batman throws his Batarangs
to cut through rope.
They are as sharp and swift
as arrows!

Batman's gas cans

blow smoke.

They can stop a bad guy cold!

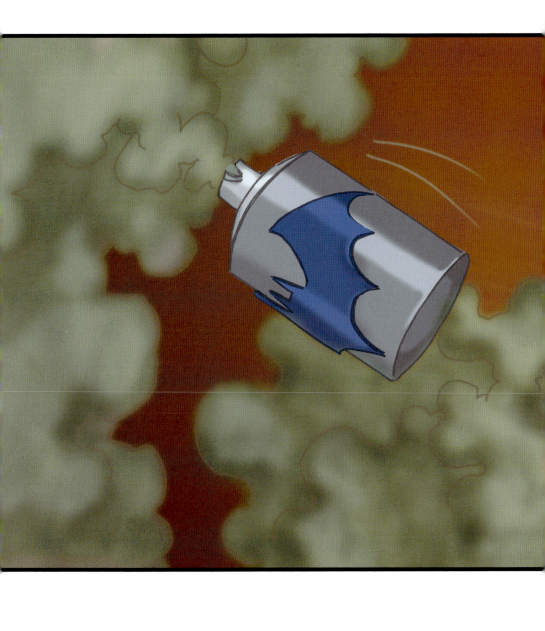

Batman's boots have steel toes.

His suit and cape can't burn.

These are no ordinary clothes!

Batman grabs his gadgets.

He is ready to roll!

BATMAN

BATMAN'S VEHICLES

Book 11 • -sh and -ch sounds

In this story you will learn about the **-ch** and **-sh** sounds. Can you find these words and sound them out?

beach	**catch**	**chase**
crash	**dash**	**each**
flash	**reach**	**screech**
search	**shadow**	**ship**

Here are some sight words:

a	**and**	**be**	**can**
for	**has**	**in**	**of**
on	**the**	**through**	**to**

Here are some fun Batman words:

climbs	**clouds**	**Batcycle**
high	**ordinary**	**soar**
vehicles		

Batman has to search

for his enemies

anytime and anywhere.

No place can be out of reach.

Batman races in the Batmobile to catch a foe on a high-speed chase.

SCREECH!

The Batcycle lets Batman

dash between cars.

Batman can soar through
the sky in a flash.
The Batplane makes a scary
shadow as it climbs through the
clouds.

The Bat-Jetski is no ordinary
boat.
It can crash through waves
and sail right up to the beach.

Each of Batman's vehicles helps

him find and catch his enemies.

Short vowel sounds:

bad	big	car
got	hidden	rich
Robin	under	up

Long vowel sounds:

Batcave	cape	deep
guys	keeps	know
no	only	secret
see	uses	

Bruce Wayne is very rich.

He's got a big house.

There is a hidden room

deep under the house.

It is the Batcave!

The Batcave is where

Bruce keeps his Batman gear.

His car, cape, and gadgets

are all there.

Batman uses the computer to see if bad guys are up to no good.

Only Alfred and Robin
know about the Batcave.

It is Batman's secret!